Make New Friends, But Keep the Old

READ MORE ADVENTURES ABOUT TWIG AND TURTLE!

TWIG AND TURTLE

Make New Friends,
But Keep the Old

Jennifer Richard Jacobson

Illustrated by Paula Franco

PIXEL ✦ INK

For Harlow Jones Jacobson

PIXEL✚INK

Text copyright © 2021 by Jennifer Richard Jacobson
Illustrations copyright © 2021 by TGM Development Corp.
All rights reserved
Pixel+Ink is a division of TGM Development Corp.
Printed and bound in March 2021 at Maple Press, York, PA, U.S.A.
Cover and interior design by Georgia Morrissey
www.pixelandinkbooks.com
Library of Congress Control Number: 2020944070
Hardcover ISBN 978-1-64595-053-0
Paperback ISBN 978-1-64595-054-7
eBook ISBN 978-1-64595-069-1
First Edition
1 3 5 7 9 10 8 6 4 2

CHAPTER
1

Today is going to be a good day.

No, not just a *good* day. A great day.

No, not just a *great* day. A stupendous day!

I decide to choose ribbons for my sneaker laces

to celebrate three things:

- It's my turn to read to Bo, the school reading
  dog.
- Angela (my best friend) and I are going to be on
  the committee to plan my class's Autumn Harvest
  Party. Our first meeting is today.

• Mom and Dad are going on a parents' vacation (okay, not so great), but Grandma is coming to stay in our tiny house! And she's going to be with us a whole week!

I'm almost ready to leave for school when I suddenly remember my bracelet. I race back upstairs and retrieve it from my shelf. Angela braided it for me. One strand of the braid is a yellow shoelace, one is a piece of twine, and one is a blue ribbon—just like the materials I thread in my sneakers depending on my moods. "No matter what you decide to lace your sneakers with, your bracelet will match!" she said when she gave it to me.

Like I said, she's my very, very best friend.

"Time for hugs!" Mom says as Turtle and I hoist

our backpacks on.

"Text Grandma some vacation cartoons!" Turtle tells Dad, who is a comic book artist.

"Text lots of pictures!" I tell Mom, who is a photographer.

"We will! We will!" they say. "And we'll video call often."

When we finally get out the door, I have a little tear growing in the corner of my left eye. But then I remind myself that Grandma will be there when we get home.

"I wonder what Grandma will bring this time?" Turtle says, as the crossing guard waves us across the street.

Grandma has a tradition of bringing supercool things. One year, she rented a karaoke machine and we spent a week belting out songs like "Let It Go" and "Girl on Fire."

Another year, she borrowed steel drums from her band. At the end of her stay, we played at a barbeque for the whole neighborhood!

"Remember the stilts?" Turtle asks.

"Ugh! How could I forget?" I say. That was last year's surprise. It took me forever to learn how to walk on them. I wanted to give up, but I knew Grandma would be disappointed. So I kept on trying and trying and trying. (Mom says that worrying about letting people down just comes with being the first-born kid in a family. Like me. And her!)

"But finally, you did it, Twig!" Turtle says.

I make a face that says *Sort of*. I took five whole steps before I went crashing over the lawn mower. But that was back in Boston. Here in Happy Trails we live in a tiny house with no lawn at all. And no

4

room for karaoke machines, or steel drums either.

When we get to the playground, Turtle spots her friends near the swings and goes racing off.

I see my friends standing by our school's front door. David and Matteo are on one side of Angela. On the other side, is a girl I don't recognize. She's wearing flowered overalls and very cool tie-up boots.

"Twig!" Angela says, pulling me over. "This is

Effie. She's going to be in our class!"

About one month ago, *I* was the new girl. I remember how hard that first day was. How alone I felt.

"You'll love it here!" I say to Effie, hoping that I'm making her feel more relaxed.

"I know," she says, and turns back to talk to Angela. "You should see how big Henry is now!"

"Is Henry your turtle, Effie?" David asks. "I remember when you brought him to school in first grade and he got loose!"

Huh?

"Mr. Kim found him in the boys' bathroom!" says Matteo.

My confusion must show, because Angela says, "Effie's family used to live here. Then they moved to Denver."

"And now we're back," says Effie.

"Hey, my Grandma's from Denver and—"

Effie's not listening. She wraps her arms around one of Angela's, like two snakes slithering down a tree, and says, "Back to Happy Trails, and back to being with my very best friend since we were three years old."

I look down at the ribbons in my sneakers.

Maybe this won't be a stupendous day after all.

CHAPTER
2

Mr. Harbor calls us to the carpet for Morning
Meeting.

I sit on one side of Angela. Effie sits on the other.
I can see that this makes Angela very happy.

"I know that many of us remember you, Effie,"
Mr. Harbor says, taking his seat. "But why don't you
tell us a few things about your year in Denver."

Effie stands up, and some kids in the room
skootch a little closer to her—like she's a powerful
living magnet. Angela looks up at her and smiles.

"In Denver, I went to a performing arts school,"
Effie says. "We performed lots of plays where I got
to grow my acting talent. I also increased my
confidence and my memorization skills."

Lots of hands shoot into the air, including mine.

"Matteo," Effie says, calling on him first.

"Were you in any plays we might know?" he asks.

"I was Elsa in *Frozen*," Effie says.

"Whoa!" everyone cries.

Yeah, wow. That sure beats singing "Let It Go" on karaoke.

Angela raises her hands and Effie calls on her—even though *other* kids have had their hands in the air longer.

"How did your memory get better?" Angela asks.

Effie rocks on her heels. "Well, I had to memorize all my lines for the play . . . and that made it easier to memorize all of my multiplication tables."

"All of them?" David asks, without being called on.

Effie nods.

Double wow. Most of us have only memorized up to our sixes.

"What's eight times nine?" David calls out.

Effie ignores David and turns to me. "Tree?" she says.

All the kids laugh.

"Her name is *Twig*, not Tree," David says.

Effie smiles. She doesn't seem to mind that she got my name wrong. That must be due to her increased confidence. "Twig?" she asks.

I want to tell her that my Grandma lives in Denver and that I did too (for a very short time), but Mr. Harbor discourages us from sharing connections. "Be curious!" he says.

So instead, I blurt, "Why did you come back?"

For some reason, this sounds as funny to my classmates as hearing me called "Tree." They laugh again.

Effie pauses, but just for a moment. "My father's top-secret job ended," she says, dramatically.

There are more *Whoas* as kids turn to look at one another, confirming Effie's star power.

"Thank you, Effie," Mr. Harbor says, signaling the

end of her time.

Effie smiles and then sits back down—right between Angela and me.

At recess, Mr. Harbor announces that the Harvest Party Committee will stay inside to plan. I grab my notebook and cluster around with the other members

13

of the committee. I love planning things. Before Grandma came, I made a long list of all the things we had to do to get ready. Here are some of the things on my list:

- Make sure Dad does laundry so Grandma has a clean towel.

- Buy her favorite almond milk.

- Squish Turtle's clothes into my drawer so Grandma can have one of her own.

- Draw a picture of Grandma's favorite flowers (purple irises) to put in Mom and Dad's loft, where she'd be sleeping.

So, I don't mind missing recess one bit. And it will give me some Angela-without-Effie time.

"Do you want to play soccer with us?" Tracy asks Effie. Tracy's looking at Effie hopefully, but Effie says, "I don't care for soccer. Besides, Angela is

trying to get me on the planning committee."

No!

"Hold on," Angela says to her. Then she goes up to Mr. Harbor, who is tidying his desk.

"Excuse me, Mr. Harbor," Angela says, talking loud enough so we can hear her. "Would it be okay if Effie joined the committee? She might have some good ideas from her other school."

Every part of me wants to jump into that conversation.

But I don't.

Here's what happens when you wish you were brave enough to share your thoughts, but you're not:

• Your throat feels like you've just swallowed a rock.

- One part of your brain practices what to say, *It wouldn't be fair to the other kids who put their name in the hat*. The other part tells you all the reasons that you should stay quiet: *Don't be mean. Don't make Angela mad. Don't make Effie an enemy.*
- Talking feels as scary and embarrassing as coming to school in your pajamas.

Mr. Harbor thinks for a moment. "I want to reconsider my decision to make this committee small," he says. "Perhaps everyone who wants to be on the committee should have the opportunity."

I want things to be fair, but not that fair, I think.

"So, for now," he says, "let's say Effie can participate *today*."

Angela walks back to us and holds up her hand to high-five Effie. But Effie grabs both of Angela's hands and jumps up and down.

The rest of us turn and settle into chairs around the reading table.

"Oh, and Twig," Mr. Harbor says, joining us. "I know today is your reading day, but I got an e-mail from Mr. Lucas."

"Mr. Lucas? Is he still the librarian?" Effie asks.

Everyone nods.

"He tells me that Mr. Kim is home sick today, so Bo won't be coming in."

"Who's Bo?" asks Effie.

"Wait until you see him!" Angela says. "He's adorable. And he loves us all so much."

I want to tell her that he's a Great Dane that used to belong to my grandmother (and me, sort of), but now he lives with Mr. Kim. He spends his days in the library listening to kids read, and he's the best dog ever.

But for some reason, that big ol' rock in my throat is still lodged there, blocking my words.

CHAPTER 3

I tell Turtle what happened at the party-planning meeting on the way home from school.

Angela suggested a game that she played at her day camp. It's called "Pumpkin Tag." If you're tagged, you have to say something you're thankful for before the tagger counts to three or you turn into a pumpkin.

"If I played, I would just think of every yummy thing that Cara makes," Turtle says. Cara has a food truck next to our tiny house, and she makes the

most amazing treats: carrot
muffins, carrot cannolis, carrot
chips, carrot fries, carrot cookies.

"You'd never be It!" I say,
since there seems to be no end
to Cara's treats. I'm hoping that
she's dropped off some for our
snack today—which she does
when she has extras.

"But it's true. I'm thankful for all of them," Turtle
says and then adds, "Pumpkin Tag sounds like a
game Mom would make up."

Truth. Our Mom is pretty big on being thankful
for all the good stuff in our lives.

"You should have suggested an acorn relay,"
Turtle says.

An acorn relay is when you try to run as fast as

you can with acorns on a spoon. Grandma taught us the game when we were little.

"I did!" I say. "But—" I start to tell her that the sort-of new girl, Effie, had the idea of making our own wooden treasure boxes covered in acorn caps. She said her dad could show us how. And that made my suggestion sound as boring as a baked potato with nothing on it. . . .

Then both Turtle and I spot something at the same time. "Grandma's van!" Turtle says. "She's here!" We can hardly wait to cross the road to see her.

Turtle races up our front porch, and I'm right behind her.

"Yikes!" says Turtle as we walk in and trip over several pairs of Grandma's shoes.

"Oh, yay! You're home!" Grandma calls from my

21

parents' loft. "I'll be right down."

Turtle gives me wide eyes as we look around.

The kitchen counters are covered with bags. On

the floor in front of the couch is a yoga mat, blocks,

and a big round pillow. Some sweaters are drying on

towels on the stairs to our loft. I head into the bathroom to find blouses hanging from the shower rod. And Grandma's big suitcase is practically blocking the toilet. I had to be a bendy acrobat to wash my hands.

Our tiny house suddenly looks tinier.

"Grandma, this place is a mess!" I hear Turtle say.

I cringe, hoping Turtle didn't hurt Grandma's feelings. I want Grandma's time with us to be *perfect*!

But Grandma just laughs as she backs down my parents' ladder and scoops Turtle into a hug.

When I get closer, she pulls me in too. She smells of lavender lotion and mint.

"I have been looking forward to this for so long!" she says.

Then she releases us and looks around. "I guess my things have taken over a bit," she says. "I'll rein them in. But first—"

Turtle jumps up and down. I jump up and down on the inside. We know what's coming.

"Surprises!" says Grandma.

Since past surprises have included machines and instruments and stilts, I expect her to go to her van. But instead, she tells us to sit up at the counter.

"Your mother must have warned me a thousand times not to bring you girls armloads of stuff—or something that wouldn't fit in this tiny house."

She glances around at the chaos. "I guess I really get it now! So," she says, poking her head into the grocery bags until she finds the right one, "I brought you these!"

From the bag, Grandma pulls out a bunch of tiny presents (teensy-tiny) and sets them down on the counter. Each one is wrapped differently. Half are for me. Half are for Turtle.

"I thought you could open one each afternoon that I'm here," Grandma says.

That's when I notice that the packages not only have our names on them, but are numbered. "Find a little number one," I say to Turtle.

Inside our first packages are tiny tattoos. Mine has itty-bitty flowers, cute little bugs, and leaves on a vine. "I'm going to make myself a tattoo bracelet just like Grandma's!" I say.

She smiles and places her hand on her wrist. I know she loves her tattoo.

"Not me!" says Turtle. "I'm putting mine on my cheeks!"

"Of course you are!" Grandma says. She gets a damp cloth and helps us apply the tattoos.

I choose my left wrist—the one that doesn't have Angela's bracelet on it.

Grandma takes her time, and the bracelet comes out looking so cute!

"I wish it wasn't temporary," I say.

"I don't think your parents would be too happy to come home and see you guys with the real things," Grandma says.

"Probably not," I say. "But maybe when we're adults."

Grandma tries to pick up her stuff, but she no sooner has some of it moved up to the loft (or back to her car) when other things appear.

She brought her deep fryer to make veggie cream cheese dumplings and her waffle iron to make

Norwegian waffles for dessert.

We eat out on the chilly porch in our cozy jackets to escape the mess in the kitchen. I don't tell Grandma that my fingers are turning into Popsicles.

"Let's work together to clean up," Grandma says, "and then we'll cuddle up and read all our favorite picture books before bed."

Turtle and I look at each other. *What do we say?*

"What?" asks Grandma. "Do you have homework

that needs to be done?"

"Not this month," I tell Grandma. "Our school is doing "No Homework November." (I hope that this is interesting enough news to distract her.)

"Wahoo!" says Grandma. "It's my lucky month. So, let's get those dishes started. Then you can get your jammies on and we'll read. We'll start with *The Prancing Dancing Ponies*!" That was Grandma's favorite when she was a little girl.

Turtle gives me a shrug. "We don't have that book, Grandma," she says.

"Yes, you do, cutie," Grandma says to Turtle as she fills the sink with lots of soapy water. "That was the very first book I gave Twig. I gave it to her before you were even born."

Turtle looks at me as if to say, *Your turn.*

I take a deep breath. "We got rid of our books

before we moved into the tiny house," I tell her.

"You just *discarded* them?" Grandma asks. "You tossed them out?"

"Oh, no!" I say. "We gave them to the shelter for homeless families—"

She stops scrubbing the batter bowl. "Your parents made the decision to have a house without books?"

"Not *without* books," Turtle says. "Just not the same books all the time."

"We get books from the library," I say.

"Or from school," Turtle adds.

"And then we return them and get different ones," I tell Grandma. "So we each only have one stack at a time."

"Because we don't have enough space," says Turtle.

Here's how you can tell that you haven't

convinced someone:

- Their eyelids droop a little, making their eyes harder to read.
- They pull their mouth over to one side.
- Their face slowly turns red.

It's Grandma's turn to take a deep breath. "So, this means no *Prancing Ponies*, no *Madeline*, no *Olivia*? What about *A Chair for My Mother*?"

"I borrowed a picture book about what they do

with the poo at the zoo," I say.

"And I have a story about monster trucks," Turtle offers.

Grandma laughs and then becomes serious again. "It still doesn't seem right that you don't have your own collection. Whenever I feel the tiniest bit lonesome, I pick up a favorite picture book."

I have to admit that I do miss having *Madeline* around all the time. "Hey!" I say, getting an idea. You can tell us the story about the Prancing Ponies. That would make us happy."

Grandma sighs. "I suppose I can," she says. "I practically know it by heart. Go get your jams on."

I have a moment of missing Mom and Dad when I'm brushing my teeth. If they were here, they would have been the ones to tell Grandma that we gave away all the books she bought us.

At least Grandma gets to tell her favorite story.

And I'll keep my feelings about Prancing Ponies to myself. Because even though it was the first book Grandma ever gave me—and I love Grandma to the moon and back—I never did like those mean ponies.

CHAPTER 4

The next day at Morning Meeting, Mr. Harbor announces that he's changed his mind about the Harvest Party committee.

Once again, Angela is sitting between Effie and me. She turns and looks at Effie. I suppose she's giving her a *Yay! You get to stay on the committee* look.

"You all work very well together," says Mr. Harbor. "You take turns talking and you listen—"

"Most of the time," David says before Mr. Harbor

gets the chance to finish his sentence.

Mr. Harbor pauses and looks at him.

"Whoops!" David says. "Sorry for interrupting."

Mr. Harbor clears his throat. "As I was saying, because you work so well together—*most of the time*—I'm going to allow everyone to join the committee. If you want to participate, stay in for recess this morning."

Effie raises her hand.

Mr. Harbor gives a little nod.

"What if you were on the committee," she says, "but changed your mind and wish to go outside instead?"

I feel like a mean prancing pony, but I'm glad that Effie doesn't want to be on the committee anymore.

Mr. Harbor rubs his chin. That means he needs to consider his answer. "Was there a conflict I should know about?" he asks Effie.

"Oh no!" she says. "I had fun planning. Angela and I just want to have some recess time this morning. We used to play a splendid game under the big pine tree"—she clasps her hands at her chest as if her name was just announced for a big award—"and we think it would be divine to play it again."

Splendid? Divine? Is Effie pretending to be someone? She sure doesn't act like any other third-grader I know.

"May I remind you all," Mr. Harbor says, "being on the committee is a responsibility. You have made a commitment to your classmates. So please make your final decisions today."

Effie bumps up and down on her bottom and

wraps her arm around Angela. Clearly, she doesn't care that she could plan this morning and play the *splendid* game during afternoon recess.

I wonder if she's thinking up ways to pull Angela away from me. Yesterday, at afternoon recess, Angela tried hard to be a friend to us both. She kept saying, "What do you think, Twig?" But I could tell that Effie wished I'd prance off and pay attention to someone else. For a moment, I'd considered finding David on the playground. David, Angela, and I are good buddies (though we've noticed that he's been hanging out with Matteo a lot lately).

Only, I wasn't ready to hand over my best friend so easily.

Angela turned toward me. "We used to play Talent Show under the tree," she says. "You can join us if you want."

Does she mean it?

Effie leans over. "But it's okay if you still want to plan for the party. You had such wonderful ideas," she says with a fake smile.

I don't know what to say. I love planning things. And we haven't even got to the fun part of planning the food and decorations.

"Don't you want to do both?" I whisper to Angela as we leave the carpet and get ready to settle into our seats for Writer's Workshop. "Plan in the morning and play in the afternoon?"

She gives me a sad face and shakes her head. "Effie called last night and made me promise that we'd play at every recess this week—before the snow really arrives and we're not allowed to play under the tree anymore."

I picture the two of them chatting away,

remembering everything they used to do together. I bet Effie has a phone just like Angela does and can talk to her anytime she wants. Without a phone (my parents won't even consider the idea until I'm in fifth grade), I hardly stand a chance in the battle over my best friend.

"But you were excited about planning," I say, giving it one more shot. "Just like me."

Angela just shrugs as if it's no big deal. "You should keep planning," she says, "if you want to."

I can't help wondering whether Angela wishes I would just go away too.

"I'll play," I

say, hope, hope, hoping that she'll say something to make me feel better.

All she says is "Okay."

I retrieve my writing binder and sit down at my desk. On top of my finished pieces is a story I wrote about the time Angela came to my house for a sleepover with Bo.

Bo! I didn't get to read to him yesterday . . . but maybe this morning? Since we're not allowed to interrupt Mr. Harbor while he's writing with us or having conferences with other students, I write him a note. He reads it between his conferences with Matteo and Tracy and glances over at me.

I must look like a girl who's about to lose her best-dog pal, because he signals me over. "Feel free to go down to the library and ask Mr. Lucas," he whispers. "But don't interrupt if he's teaching. Come right back."

I grab my latest book choice and practically skip to the library.

Fortunately, Mr. Lucas is sitting at his desk. I glance at Bo's cozy corner where kids cuddle up with him, but he's not there. My excitement sags. He must be out walking with Mr. Kim.

"Hi, Mr. Lucas," I say when he looks up from his book catalog.

Mr. Lucas is startled. "Twig!"

Then I hear a big thumping . . . and an enormous rustling!

"Hold on!" Mr. Lucas says, reaching down. But Bo is already poking his head out from under Mr. Lucas's desk to say hello to me!

Within moments, he's skootched his whole body out and is giving me one of his biggest hellos!

"Down, Bo!" I say, because I don't want him to

forget his good library manners.

Mr. Lucas tells me that Bo is free for twenty minutes of listening.

Listening! Just what I need. So even though I have a book in my hand, I don't read. Instead, I tell Bo all about Effie and how I think I'm losing my best friend.

That's when Bo gives me a giant lick on my face as if to remind me that he was my best friend before Angela.

"Of course!" I say. It feels good to be reminded that I have lots of friends: Bo, Angela, David, Matteo.

Even my sister is a good friend. Maybe I can make room for one more?

Maybe.

CHAPTER 5

Maybe *not*.

Maybe I can't make room for one more friend. At least not one more who is actually a mean prancing pony in disguise.

It appears that the splendid game of Talent Show is beginning.

Effie welcomes the audience. Which is only me, sitting on the crunchy, cold, grass. (Practically everyone else is inside planning the party.)

Then she introduces Angela, the co-host of

Talent Show.

Effie says to Angela, "Remember when you made up that dance and then I joined you and we kept getting wilder and wilder. We fell on the ground laughing, and we couldn't even stop!"

Angela remembers and laughs. Effie does a little dance wiggle and Angela laughs harder.

David comes over to sit next to me. "Hey," he says.

"Hey," I say back, giving him my *I'm so glad to see you* smile.

That's when Effie pulls Angela over to the sidelines because she, Effie the Songbird, is the first talent onstage.

I think we'll probably hear a show tune, but instead she sings a song that tells a complicated story, only it sounds like she's making it up as she goes along.

And goes along. And goes along.

David says, "This is boring. Do you want to kick the soccer ball around?"

I do. But I can't explain it. I feel like if I get up

now and do something else, I will have given in. Or given up. Given up on having a best girlfriend. "I'm going to see what Angela does," I say.

David gives me a little look that says *Not me* and heads off.

The bell rings before Angela gets her turn.

When Turtle and I arrive home that afternoon, the house is filled with more Grandma stuff: watercolor paints on the counter, weights on the floor, gardening books on the staircase. But Grandma is nowhere in sight.

It's weird to be the only two home. We've never walked into an empty (well, not so empty) house before. I can't help thinking that something must be wrong. I glance around for Grandma's hiking shoes. Here in Happy Trails, people get lost on the mountains all the time.

I try not to let Turtle know that I'm worried.

Just as I'm about to suggest we talk to Cara, Grandma bursts through the door. "You beat me home!" she says. "I was delivering Norwegian waffles to Mr. Bryant."

Mr. Bryant is the owner of Sudsy's Laundromat, which is right next door. He let my parents turn his back room into a work studio. We all like hanging out there . . . even Grandma, I guess.

"You scared me, Grandma!" Turtle says. "I thought you were lost somewhere!"

"Oh, no!" Grandma takes Turtle's hands in hers and looks right into her eyes. "Why would you think that?"

I don't tell Grandma that I was thinking the very same thing.

Grandma serves us waffles with lingonberry jam, and we open presents number two.

Inside our packages are adorable little books. The covers are spin art—mine is green and gold. Nature-like. Twig-like.

"They're inspiration journals!" Grandma says. "This afternoon, we can take a walk, and I want you to record ten things in your book that you've never noticed before. Then we'll come back and write poems!"

Turtle looks skeptical. "Grandma, my words won't fit in this little book."

Grandma thinks for a minute. "What if you draw pictures?"

Turtle spreads her arms wide. "I like to do things

BIG, Grandma. I like to
write BIG. I like to draw
BIG."

I think of Grandma
going to all the effort to give us
tiny presents, and I'm afraid
she's feeling sad. I wish
Turtle would just *try* to draw
tiny.

"But I'll see new things,"
Turtle says, "and *you* can write the words in my
book, Grandma."

Grandma doesn't look satisfied with that.

"That way, I'll learn the words!" Turtle adds.

Grandma smiles. She sees that the book will be
meaningful to Turtle after all.

We finish our waffles and head out on our walk.

Which is really fun. Even though Turtle and I go the same way to and from school, there are lots of things I've never noticed before. Here are the first five:

- Diamond pattern on the tires of Cara's truck
- Crack in the sidewalk that forms a perfect "T" for Twig (and Turtle, of course)
- Hole in the side of the oak tree in front of Mrs. Wallaby's Toy Store (Does an animal live in there?)
- Crooked sign on the Vintage Store
- Nest over the library door

I write down *diamond*, *crack*, *hole*, *sign*, and *nest*.

I'm squatting down on the library lawn, looking at what's probably a chipmunk hole, when I hear familiar voices.

I look up, and who do I see? Effie the Songbird. She's walking next to someone who I'm guessing is her grandfather, and she's carrying a tall stack of books. Just as they pass my grandma, Effie's stack starts to topple.

"Whoa!" Grandma says and catches the books before they hit the ground.

"Oh my! Thank you!" Effie says to Grandma. I wonder if she's even noticed me.

"Happy to help," says Grandma. She introduces herself to Effie's grandfather and says she's visiting from Denver. Turtle, who is always curious about new things, stands next to Grandma.

"Joe Hunter," the man says. "Effie, here, just came from Denver herself!"

"You must be the same age as my granddaughter," Grandma says. "Twig! Come meet Effie." She starts to say that I'm practically a new girl as well when Effie interrupts.

"Twig and I are in the same class in school. She welcomed me already. But I'm not as new as she is. I used to live here before."

I stand and reluctantly walk over. I have barely

nodded a hi before my grandma says, "Why don't you plan on coming over on Sunday afternoon, Effie? The two of you girls can have a playdate."

"That sounds like fun," Effie's grandfather says.

Effie smiles. "Thank you, Mrs. Goodale. I'd love that," she says.

I'm shocked. Totally shocked. That is, until she adds . . .

"Would it be all right to bring my friend Angela too?"

CHAPTER 6

We have a video call with Mom and Dad on Saturday. Grandma sets up the laptop, and then tells us that she'll be right next door at Sudsy's. "Come and find me when you're done," she says.

"Don't you want to talk to them?" I ask.

"I got to chat with your mom yesterday when you were in school," Grandma says. "This is your special time to catch up." She reminds me how to accept the call and heads out the door.

"Do you think Mr. Bryant is Grandma's new

boyfriend?" Turtle asks.

"No . . . I don't think so. . . ." I say to Turtle.
But maybe she's right. Grandma is acting awfully
strange. As if she has a secret. And it's not like her
to pass up a chance to talk with Mom—even if she
did talk with her yesterday.

Ding!

"There they are!" Turtle says as our parents' faces
appear on the screen.

At first, everyone is talking at once! Mom and Dad want to hear everything we've been doing, and we want to hear all about their vacation.

"You go!" they say.

"No, you go!" we say.

Turtle tells them about the little daily gifts. Today's presents were packages of bookplates. "Those are stickers," Turtle explains. "Mine say: *This book belongs to Turtle McKay.* You're supposed to put them inside the cover of your books, so everyone knows who they belong to."

"Grandma didn't realize that we don't have our books anymore," I tell them.

Mom pulls the corners of her mouth down—her *oh, no* face.

"But I said we could draw on them and stick them up on our walls!" Turtle says.

"Did Grandma suggest you wait until we're home before doing that?" Dad asks.

Turtle nods. "She said just decorate them for now."

We hear about the trip: hiking in canyon slots and eating campfire beans. And then Mom asks, "Are you okay, Twig? You seem awfully quiet this morning."

"I was just thinking," I say. And then I add, "There's a new girl at school."

"Her name is Effie," Turtle says.

"Another friend in Happy Trails!" Dad exclaims.

I wish it felt that simple. Part of me wants to tell them that I'm not gaining a friend. In fact, I may very well be losing one. But I know Mom especially will worry about me. And I don't want her worrying on her vacation.

"Grandma invited Effie and Angela over for a

playdate tomorrow afternoon," I say. I hope I've kept the little bit of dread I'm feeling out of my voice.

"That sounds fun!" Mom says. "Remember the details so you can tell me all about it."

I agree, hoping that I'll have some happy details to share.

After the call, we head next door to the laundromat as planned. Mr. Bryant is in the front, helping a customer look for a missing sock. "Your grandma's in the back room," he says to us, smiling.

We walk into Mom's and Dad's studio, but it definitely isn't the way Mom and Dad left it. Their computers and worktables are covered in sheets. In the center of the room is a ground cloth. And on the ground cloth are two sawhorses. Grandma is standing over a piece of wood, sawing.

She finishes cutting and looks up to find us there.

"Nice goggles, Grandma!" Turtle says.

"Mr. Bryant leant them to me," she says, sliding them up on her forehead. "Along with the tools."

I look closely at Grandma's project. "Are you building a bookcase?"

Grandma nods. "Surprise! I got permission from Mr. Bryant and your parents. I'm building you a small library in the corner of this room."

"But where will we get the books?" Turtle asks.

"We can buy some at the used book store," I suggest. There are always a few kids' books on the shelves.

"And at Threadbare Binding Bookstore!" says Grandma.

Turtle and I just look at our grandmother. Neither of us have heard of that place.

"It's the best little bookstore two towns over," Grandma says. "That's my other surprise. We're heading over there today so you can pick out a few favorites. Favorites that you'll want to keep around forever!"

"Like *Goodnight Moon* and *Flossie & the Fox*?" asks Turtle.

"Sure!" Grandma says.

"And then we can use our bookplates!" I say.

"That's right, Twig. So, if you lend your books to a friend, they always find their way home."

Grandma places the board on top of the bookcase. "Here, Turtle," she says. "You can help me hold this board in place.

She slips off the goggles and hands them to me. "Slide these on, Twig. Then pick up that hammer and a nail. You can pound the top in place."

We have a maker station in our library at school. Mr. Lucas helped me practice pounding nails into a board without hitting my finger. It's fun.

I choose a nail from the pile and carefully line it up. I'm about to lower the hammer when Grandma says, "Oh and don't worry, Twig. I called the book-store. They have a copy of *The Prancing Dancing Ponies* and they're holding it for you!"

CHAPTER 7

Grandma's van looks a lot like our tiny house while she's visiting. On the front seat are a bird-watching book, an idea journal, a sweater, some CDs, and a water bottle. On the back seats are more clothes, bug repellant, sunscreen, drumsticks, a blanket, and a small cooler with snacks. And a few granola-bar wrappers that haven't made it into her trash bag.

The van smells like wool and Grandma's orange ChapStick.

Grandma quickly sweeps off the seats to belt in our boosters—then us.

The ride to Threadbare Binding is pretty, with lots of hills and pine trees to look at. Grandma tells us that we can each pick out two old favorites and one new book to begin our library. Turtle and I immediately begin thinking of books we loved.

We remember some books that made us feel cozy, and some that made our mouths drop open in surprise. We had funny books that we'd ask Mom or Dad to read over and over again, and we'd laugh every time.

By the time we get to the bookstore, I can't wait to get inside and see which of our old friends they have.

We head down some stairs and into the coolest children's area. There's a playhouse with cushions inside. And all around are different-sized chairs for finding the just right seat. Where to begin?

Turtle has found *Goodnight Moon*. I hope she chooses this as one of her old friends. It's one of my favorites too. (We were always trying to guess what kind of mush was in that bowl.) If she chooses that one, I can choose two others.

Or can I? Do I only get one old friend since the store is saving *The Prancing Dancing Ponies* for me? My stomach sinks a little.

I think of Grandma loving that story. *(Why?)* And how she bought it for me when I was just a baby. And now she's built the bookshelves so we can share those books we all love. I suppose I can let Grandma buy it and be happy because it reminds me of her.

But I don't want to. I don't want to own a book about three ponies who dress as princesses and then hurt someone's feelings. And I don't want to leave with just two books that I like.

"Look what I have!" Grandma singsongs as she comes around the corner. She's holding up that mean book and strutting like a dancing pony.

She's so funny, and so happy, I can't help smiling.

"All yours, sweetheart," she says as she places it in my hands.

Then she waltzes off to see what Turtle is choosing.

I open the cover and peek inside. Maybe those ponies only seemed mean to me because I was so little. Maybe they were being funny, and I didn't get it. I open to the back pages of this book. You can tell that it was published a long time ago. There are more words than typical, and some of the pictures are in black and white. I reread the ending.

Nope! I slam the cover shut. Those ponies are still hurting feelings.

And then I get an idea. What if I were to accidentally set this book down? I move closer to another family checking out books on a display rack. "Excuse me," I say and slip *The Prancing Dancing Ponies* on the rack in front of them. Maybe one of those kids will decide that they just have to own this horse book. If so, I'll apologize to Grandma for being careless.

I turn, and the room suddenly feels dark to me. I imagine the books marching forward, accusing me of abandoning their friend.

I try to ignore them and look for a happy familiar title. It doesn't take long. *Blueberries for Sal* practically jumps off the shelf and into my hands. I love Sal, picking her blueberries alongside a baby bear!

Next, I look for a new book. One I haven't read before.

Turtle wanders over to me. "Look at this one, Twig!" she says. It's about a boy named Jabari who's trying to be brave enough to jump off the high diving board.

"That looks like a good one," I say and go back to my looking. I find a nonfiction book about trees, and then *Alma and How She Got Her Name.* I want this book so badly, too, since everyone is always asking me how I got the name Twig.

Grandma appears by our side with three adult books. "Time for final choices!" she says. "I have another surprise planned."

I stand there frozen, waiting for her to notice (or maybe not notice?) the three books in my arms.

She takes the pile from me and examines the titles. "Wait!" she says, spinning around the room. She spies the pony book on the display rack and brings it back to me. "Someone must have shelved this while you were looking for others!"

I force a small smile.

Grandma fans my books out. "Which one goes

71

back?" she asks.

In that moment, I decide that if Jabari can be brave enough to jump off the high dive, I can tell my grandmother how I really feel.

"Grandma . . ." My voice is too quiet to hear. I try again.

"Grandma . . ."

She stops inspecting Turtle's choices and looks at me.

"Grandma, I love you and I love our new library, but I do not love *The Prancing Dancing Ponies*!" I want to stop there, but now that I've spoken the truth, I can't seem to hold my words back. "I don't want it," I say.

Grandma looks stunned.

"I don't want to hurt your feelings. But those ponies are mean!"

"Oh my goodness!" Grandma says, looking at me.

I can't tell if she is reacting to my behavior or to
what I've confessed. I just wait.

She leads me back to a table. "Come show me,
Twig."

I turn to the back pages and point out the nastiness.

"My goodness!" she says again. "You're absolutely
right! I guess I got all caught up in the silliness of the
horses dressing up in beautiful gowns and making
their way into the city. Let's put this book back. You

73

pick out one that makes you happy."

I show her *Blueberries for Sal*, still in my arms.

"Oh, I love that book too!" she says.

I have no idea where my first copy came from. "Did you give this to me when I was a baby?" I ask.

"I'm not sure," Grandma says. "But I'm so happy to be buying it for you now."

Suddenly the room feels brighter, airier. The bright colors on the spines of the books dance around the room. I'm so happy I spoke up. So glad I told the truth. I promise myself that I won't be afraid to speak up next time.

Our next stop is an ice cream shop that has thirty-two flavors of homemade deliciousness.

We all get cones. Mine is piled high with chocolate cherry chunk.

"Girls," Grandma says, between licks. "I want you to know that you can always tell me what's on your mind."

"Even if we hurt your feelings?" I ask.

Grandma thinks for a moment. "If what you have to say is said with kindness, then I would like to hear it."

I take a bite of my ice cream, feeling relieved.

"Grandma, I'm so glad you're visiting us," Turtle says.

"Why thank you," Grandma says, smiling.

"But you are too messy!" Turtle adds. "Your stuff takes up the whole house!"

I look at Grandma. Did Turtle say that kindly enough?

Grandma throws her head back and laughs.

Then the three of us laugh so hard we can hardly eat our cones.

"I understand your point. I'm going to work on that, Turtle," she says.

Later that night, after we've read four of our new books and Turtle is brushing her teeth, Grandma says to me, "I've been thinking about our talk today, Twig. It occurred to me that sometimes, keeping your thoughts to yourself might mean that you don't trust the other person to care about your feelings."

I have to think about that for a moment. Then I

shake my head. "I trust you, Grandma!"

"Good," she says, giving me a hug. "Because I will always care about your feelings, sweetie. Always."

"Thank you," I say, giving her a big hug back.

I fall asleep thinking about what Grandma said and wondering if, perhaps, there is a place in my life where I'm not trusting someone to care about my feelings.

And speaking up will take a whole lot more bravery than I showed today.

CHAPTER 8

Grandma joins me at the counter, where I'm eating granola for breakfast and making a list of activities that Angela and Effie and I can do this afternoon. I love planning.

Here's what's on my list so far:

- Go on a nature walk and collect things to make fairy houses.

- Play hopscotch on the sidewalk.

- Make a village out of playing cards.

- Draw pictures with our eyes closed.

• Play Monopoly.

"Are you excited to have friends over today?" Grandma asks.

I slowly nod. I want Grandma to think of me as a happy girl—one with lots of friends. But then I think, *You're still holding back, Twig!* So I add, "Angela and I met in Social Skills Club. That's a club that helps kids make friends. We've been friends—along with our other friend, David—ever since. But lately, David's been playing with Matteo, and now Effie's come back to town. She and Angela have been BFFs since they were three!" I sigh. It feels too hard to go on.

Grandma nods. "And now you're afraid of losing Angela," she says.

I twist the bracelet on my wrist, the one that Angela gave to me. "She's really fun—and thoughtful. And I don't want to have to find an FBF."

80

"FBF?" Grandma says, scrunching her forehead.

"Future best friend," I tell her.

"Hmm. Maybe Effie can be your FBF," Grandma says. "I'll admit, it might be harder to be friends with both girls, but certainly not impossible."

I want to tell Grandma that even if *I* think that's a good idea, Effie and Angela might not. But I don't have to tell her. The way she looks at me tells me she already knows.

She takes my empty bowl to the sink. Normally, it's Turtle's and my job to wash dishes, but Grandma says that Mom and Dad's vacation can be our vacation too. (That, and she's practicing being neater.)

Turtle comes in from outside. She's soaking wet.

"It's raining?" I stop to listen. Sure enough, there's a patter on our roof that quickly turns into drumming.

Turtle looks down at my sheet of paper. A drop of water runs off her forehead and onto the page. "What are you writing?" she asks.

"I'm devising a plan for fun. What were you doing out in the rain?" I ask.

"Checking to see if there were puddles yet. I want to go puddle jumping!"

I sigh. "This day isn't turning out the way I hoped," I say, crossing the two outdoor activities off my list.

"What do these say?" Turtle asks, pointing to the three that I haven't crossed off. Her finger makes another wet splotch.

"Drawing, Monopoly, and card village," I say, knowing how boring and "un-splendid" they sound.

"You could add playing Magic Woods," she says.

I think about that. Turtle and I love playing Magic Woods. But not every third-grader loves pretend games. Effie might think that it's babyish. Turtle looks hopeful. Like we might include her too.

"*Maybe*," I say with a little smile. "But no promises!"

Grandma has errands to run, so Turtle and I hang out in the studio where Mr. Bryant can keep an eye on us. We place our new books on the shelves and talk about ways of earning money so we can buy more.

"Let's look in the dryers!" Turtle says. She's always finding coins that have fallen out of people's pockets.

After Grandma comes home and we've eaten lunch, Angela and Effie arrive.

They pull up in the same car together. I feel a pang of jealousy. Were they together all morning? Grandma waves to Angela's mother from the porch. Neither grown-up wants to venture into the rain to say hello.

"Your house is so adorable!" Effie says as she peels off her raincoat. Fortunately, Grandma has moved most of her random stuff to the car. There are only a few things that she purchased this morning scattered on the couch now.

Grandma gives me a little eyebrow raise that seems to say *"So far so good."* She takes both their wet coats to hang in the shower stall and says, "Give them a tour, Twig."

"I'll give the tour!" says Turtle, eager to be involved.

I step aside so she can lead the way. I don't mind. I'm feeling shy, and Turtle loves giving tours.

Turtle begins in the kitchen. She shows Effie and Angela (who is pretending that she's seeing everything for the first time too) how our cutting board fits over our kitchen sink (now there's more counter space!) and how our shelves on the wall not only hold things on top of them but below too. (Mom and Dad used super-strong glue to hang jars with lids under the shelves, for holding more stuff.)

"I want to do that in my room!" Effie says.

I can't believe how nice she's being. Maybe I was just imagining a problem between us.

Next, Turtle leads everyone up to our loft.

"You get to sleep in sleeping bags all the time?" Effie asks.

"Aren't they lucky?" Angela says. "They're so cozy."

"And it's easy to make the beds!" I say, showing them how all you have to do is give them one good lift into the air to straighten them out.

Only Effie isn't really watching.

"You have cooking pots in your room?" she asks, looking at our shelves.

Her voice sounds less nice.

Turtle lifts the lid off one. "Ta-da!" she says, showing Effie that the pots hold our toys.

"She is so adorable!" Effie says to Angela. Then she turns to me. "I didn't know you had the cutest little sister."

Turtle doesn't like being called *little* or *cute*. She makes a face behind Effie's back and heads down-stairs.

I think of speaking up, of saying that, but my mouth suddenly forgets how to work.

"Is this the end of the tour?" Angela asks.

"I guess so," I say. "You can see my parents' loft over there there, and the living room is below us. The bathroom is in the back."

"What can we do?" Effie asks. "There doesn't seem to be much to play with."

I perk up. "I made a list of fun—"

Just then, we hear music.

"What's that?" Effie asks, peering over the railing.

I explain that Turtle's dancing to her favorite video.

"*Dance Like a Flamingo!*" Angela says.

Effie grabs Angela's arm. "Let's do that!" she says.

Angela turns and starts down the stairs.

I wonder if Grandma's listening to what's going

on. If she is, I can't tell. She's climbing the ladder to my parents' loft. Nevertheless, I can still remember her words: *A good host makes sure the guests have a good time.* She used to tell us that when neighborhood kids visited us in Denver.

So I head down to dance like a flamingo. It's not my favorite thing, but at least I can relax knowing that Effie and Angela are having fun.

Turtle, who gets in the flamingo zone, hardly notices that we've joined her.

Effie grabs Angela's arms and they do the whole dance without letting go of each other. Effie looks like she's performing on-stage.

That leaves me off to the side. I flap my wings, but I don't feel much like flying.

After the video ends, I make a suggestion. "Want to play Monopoly? Or draw comics with our eyes closed?" I ask.

Effie makes a *definitely not* face. "Angela and I like to do things like put on fancy dress-up clothes and makeup," she says.

Turtle and I don't have a dress-up box. Sometimes, we go over to Sudsy's and dress up in the clothes that have been left in the lost and found. But something tells me that Effie wouldn't find that fun.

Maybe Grandma has some clothes we can try on? I'm not sure how Grandma will feel about that . . . and she hardly wears any makeup at all.

Effie turns to Angela. "Maybe Twig's grandma can drive us over to your house to play? You have so many fun toys."

Angela looks at me.

"You guys figure it out," Effie says. "I have to go to the powder room."

Not bathroom.

Powder room.

Now it's just

Angela and me.

We seem to be

frozen in place.

It seems like we

just look at each other

forever.

But it's clear.

One of us has to speak up.

CHAPTER
9

"Do you want to go to your house?" I ask Angela.

She just shrugs.

Be brave, I tell myself. *Be brave, like Jabari.* "Do you still want to be my friend?" I whisper to Angela. "Because it feels like you want Effie to be your one-and-only friend."

There. I've said it. No taking it back.

Here's what someone does when what you've said is right:

• They give a little nod.

- Their mouth turns down, but you know they're secretly relieved.

- They let you keep talking.

Angela does none of those things. She grabs my arm and says, "No! I don't want that!"

And I just know she means it.

She whispers, "Effie's family is going through a hard time right now. My mom wants me to help her feel at home again."

Oh. I feel better. (And a little closer to Effie at the same time.) I could just let it go. But I figure this is my chance to say everything that is on my mind. "I can't help it," I say. "I'm feeling left out. I don't have memories with Effie. I haven't played the same games. It's like I'm"—I search for the right word—*"discarded."*

Angela makes a sad face. "Oh, sorry!" she says.

She starts to give me a hug when Effie comes back into the room.

"Shouldn't we get our raincoats?" Effie asks.

"No," Angela says. "I think we should stay here. Twig always has fun stuff to do. Let's try drawing with our eyes closed."

"Why?" asks Effie. "It sounds stupid."

Maybe, I think, *Effie doesn't like doing things she's not good at.*

"I know it sounds silly," I tell her. "But one of the best things about this game is that everyone can do it—and no one is very good at it."

She sighs. "I guess we can try it."

"Can I play?" Turtle asks.

Part of me would like it to just be the three of us, but another part of me knows that it's no fun to be left out. "Sure," I say.

Grandma comes down from the loft. "Would you like some help setting up the table?" she asks.

"I can do it!" Turtle says. It's one of her favorite things about the tiny house.

"Would you like to play, Grandma?" I ask.

She thinks for a moment. "How about I make waffles while you play?"

"Yes, please!" Angela says.

Grandma lends us her phone so we can time three minutes for each drawing.

First, everyone closes their eyes and draws a bird.

The timer goes off and I open my eyes. Ha ha! My bird looks like a lumpy camel with a jagged nose.

Effie laughs and shows her silly drawing. She tried to draw a bird flying, but it looks more like a star with teeth.

We all look at Angela's.

"Angela," says Turtle. "Birds don't have four legs."

"They don't?" Angela thinks for a minute and then bursts into laughter. "I don't know why, but I imagined that they did."

This is how the game goes. We take turns choosing what everyone will draw. Effie suggests mermaids and unicorns. Angela suggests spaceships and bikes (really hard!). Turtle suggests leopards with spots and monster trucks. I suggest a soccer player and a tree. Even though our eyes are closed, we all draw awesome trees!

Grandma serves us waffles and asks about the planning for the Autumn Harvest Party.

"Who cares," says Effie. "Every year we do boring things—like playing acorn tag."

"If you're talking about the acorn relay, then that was my idea. And it hurts my feelings to hear you make fun of it," I say, just like that.

Grandma gives me a little *attagirl* tap on my shoulder as she walks by. She's setting up her yoga mat.

"Sorry," Effie says. "It's just . . . stupid."

Angela and I look at each other. Effie doesn't sound sorry. And I hadn't realized until now that *stupid* is one of her favorite words.

"Twig said you were going to make treasure boxes,"

Turtle says. "They sound cool."

Effie folds her arms over her chest. "My dad can't help us. He says he has to spend all his time looking for a job now." Suddenly, she no longer looks like the confident girl who stood at the front of the room and told us about her performing arts school. She looks like a crumpled leaf.

"Nothing feels the same in my life," she adds with a sigh.

Maybe that's why Effie doesn't want to plan anymore.

"I know what you mean," I say. "That's how I felt when we had to move two times this fall."

"You moved twice?" Effie asks.

"I moved from Boston to Denver. And then from Denver to here."

"You were in Denver?" she asks as if she's really interested this time.

We talk about the things we love in Denver—even Angela, who has visited there many times, chimes in.

Grandma plunks down on her mat.

"Can we do yoga with you?" Angela asks her.

"Sure!" Grandma says.

"You really want to do *that*?" I ask her. Turtle and I never do yoga with Grandma.

"Yes! Let's try it!" she says.

Effie and I look at each other and shrug. Then we smile. It's our first *just us* smile.

While we're doing Downward Dog, I peek at Effie through my legs and ask, "Do you remember how to make a treasure box?"

"Sort of," she says.

"Maybe you could talk to Mr. Lucas and he could help us make them. It wouldn't be as good as having your dad, but it might be really fun."

She's quiet for a moment. I think she might tell me that it's a stupid idea. But she doesn't.

"Why don't we all talk to Mr. Lucas?" she says. "Then, at the Harvest Party, we can work the table together!"

"Great idea!" Angela and I say at the same time.

We finish yoga, and Grandma picks up her mat and a couple of the packages on the couch.

"I don't know why I bought all of this embroidery thread," she says, holding up a bunch of it. "I'm really not the sort of person who has the patience for little stitches. I'm more like Turtle. I like to work on big things!"

"Do you like big things like puddle jumping?" Turtle asks.

Grandma laughs. "Why not?" she says.

Grandma and Turtle put on rain gear. I'm relieved that neither of my friends suggests we join them. Puddle jumping is not my thing.

"What do you want to do now?" I ask my friends as we stretch out on the couch.

"What else is on your list?" Effie asks.

As I pull the list from my pocket, I notice something. I notice the bracelet on my wrist. The one that Angela gave me. And it gives me a good idea.

"Want to make bracelets?" I ask. "We can use the thread that Grandma bought but doesn't really want."

"Sure!" Effie and Angela say at the very same time.

"Are you sure your grandmother won't mind?" Angela asks.

I nod. I'm certain of it.

We each choose three colors and begin braiding them.

"Hey," says Effie. "What if we each made a braid for one another and . . ."

"And we wove them together," Angela says, "to . . ."

"Make friendship bracelets!" I say.

And that's exactly what we do.

For a few moments we are perfectly, happily quiet while we weave.

And that's okay.

Because sometimes, good friends don't need to say a thing.

HAMSTER
ERASERS

TATTOOS

BOOKPLATES

7
TiNY PRESENTS
FROM GRANDMA

JOURNALS

PET ROCKS TO PAINT

FINGER PUPPETS

MYSTERY JELLY BEANS

Don't miss more Twig and Turtle Adventures

TWiG AND TURTLE

1

Big Move to a Tiny House

JENNiFER RiCHARD JACOBSON

Illustrated by Paula Franco

TWIG AND TURTLE

2

Toy Store Trouble

JENNIFER RICHARD JACOBSON

Illustrated by Paula Franco

TWIG AND TURTLE

3

Quiet Please!

JENNIFER RICHARD JACOBSON

Illustrated by Paula Franco

ABOUT THE AUTHOR

JENNIFER RICHARD JACOBSON is the award-winning author of many books for children and young adults, including the Andy Shane early-reader series and her most recent book, *The Dollar Kids*. A graduate of Harvard Graduate School of Education, when not writing, Jennifer provides trainings in Writer's Workshop for teachers. Jennifer lives in Maine with her husband and dog.